MR HUMPHREYS AND HIS INHERITANCE

-FANTASY AND HORROR CLASSICS-

BY

M. R. JAMES

British Library Cataloguing-in-Publication Data
A catalogue record for this book is available from the
British Library

M. R. James

Montague Rhodes James was born in Kent, England in 1862. An intellectually gifted child, he excelled academically at both Temple Grove School and Eton College before enrolling at King's College, Cambridge. A highly respected scholar to this day, James' areas of research interest were apocryphal Biblical literature and mediaeval illuminated manuscripts. He was, by turns, Fellow, Dean, and Tutor at King's College, and in 1905 was installed as Provost. James was a highly sociable man, and he travelled widely throughout Europe.

James came to writing fiction relatively late, not publishing his first collection of short stories – Ghost Stories of an Antiquary (1904) – until the age of 42. Many of his tales were written as Christmas Eve entertainments and read aloud to friends. James described his introduction to ghosts in 1931: "In my childhood I chanced to see a toy Punch and Judy set, with figures cut out in cardboard. One of these was The Ghost. It was a tall figure habited in white with an unnaturally long and narrow head, also surrounded with white, and a dismal visage. Upon this my conceptions of a ghost were based, and for years it permeated my dreams." James believed that must a good story must "put the reader into the position of saying to himself: 'If I'm not careful, something of this kind may happen to me!'" He eventually published five collections of his ghost stories, all of which were reprinted and adapted numerous times.

Modern scholars now see James as having redefined the ghost story for the 20th century by abandoning many of the formal Gothic clichés of his predecessors and using more realistic contemporary settings. However, James's tales tend to reflect his own antiquarian interests, and he is seen as the founder of the 'antiquarian ghost story'. His first two collections – Ghost Stories of an Antiquary (1904) and More Ghost Stories (1911) – are generally regarded as his most important, containing as they do the well-known stories 'Number 13', 'Count Magnus', 'Oh, Whistle and I'll Come to You, My Lad' and 'Casting the Runes'.

The onset of World War One marked the beginning of the end of James' golden years in Cambridge. In 1918, he accepted the post of Provost of Eton College. He was awarded the Order of Merit in 1930, and died in 1936, aged 73.

MR HUMPHREYS AND HIS INHERITANCE

About fifteen years ago, on a date late in August or early in September, a train drew up at Wilsthorpe, a country station in Eastern England. Out of it stepped (with other passengers) a rather tall and reasonably good-looking young man, carrying a handbag and some papers tied up in a packet. He was expecting to be met, one would say, from the way in which he looked about him: and he was, as obviously, expected. The stationmaster ran forward a step or two, and then, seeming to recollect himself, turned and beckoned to a stout and consequential person with a short round beard who was scanning the train with some appearance of bewilderment. 'Mr. Cooper,' he called out,—'Mr. Cooper, I think this is your gentleman'; and then to the passenger who had just alighted, 'Mr. Humphreys, sir? Glad to bid you welcome to Wilsthorpe. There's a cart from the Hall for your luggage, and here's Mr. Cooper, what I think you know.' Mr. Cooper had hurried up, and now raised his hat and shook hands. 'Very pleased, I'm sure,' he said, 'to give the echo to Mr. Palmer's kind words. I should have been the first to render expression to them but for the face not being familiar to me, Mr. Humphreys. May your residence among us be marked as a red-letter day, sir.' 'Thank you very much, Mr. Cooper,' said Humphreys, 'for your good wishes, and Mr. Palmer also. I do hope very much that this change of—er—

tenancy—which you must all regret, I am sure—will not be to the detriment of those with whom I shall be brought in contact.' He stopped, feeling that the words were not fitting themselves together in the happiest way, and Mr. Cooper cut in, 'Oh, you may rest satisfied of that, Mr. Humphreys. I'll take it upon myself to assure you, sir, that a warm welcome awaits you on all sides. And as to any change of propriety turning out detrimental to the neighbourhood, well, your late uncle—' And here Mr. Cooper also stopped, possibly in obedience to an inner monitor, possibly because Mr. Palmer, clearing his throat loudly, asked Humphreys for his ticket. The two men left the little station, and—at Humphreys' suggestion—decided to walk to Mr. Cooper's house, where luncheon was awaiting them.

The relation in which these personages stood to each other can be explained in a very few lines. Humphreys had inherited—quite unexpectedly—a property from an uncle: neither the property nor the uncle had he ever seen. He was alone in the world—a man of good ability and kindly nature, whose employment in a Government office for the last four or five years had not gone far to fit him for the life of a country gentleman. He was studious and rather diffident, and had few out-of-door pursuits except golf and gardening. To-day he had come down for the first time to visit Wilsthorpe and confer with Mr. Cooper, the bailiff, as to the matters which needed immediate attention. It may be asked how this came to be his first visit? Ought he not in decency to have attended his uncle's funeral? The answer is not far to seek: he had been abroad at the time of the death, and his address had not been at once procurable. So he had put off coming to Wilsthorpe till he heard that all things were ready for him. And now we find him arrived at Mr. Cooper's comfortable house, facing the parsonage, and having just shaken hands with the smiling Mrs. and Miss Cooper.

During the minutes that preceded the announcement of luncheon the party settled themselves on elaborate chairs in the drawing-room, Humphreys, for his part, perspiring quietly in the consciousness that stock was being taken of him.

'I was just saying to Mr. Humphreys, my dear,' said Mr. Cooper, 'that I hope and trust that his residence among us here in Wilsthorpe will be marked as a red-letter day.'

'Yes, indeed, I'm sure,' said Mrs. Cooper heartily, 'and many, many of them.'

Miss Cooper murmured words to the same effect, and Humphreys attempted a pleasantry about painting the whole calendar red, which, though greeted with shrill laughter, was evidently not fully understood. At this point they proceeded to luncheon.

'Do you know this part of the country at all, Mr. Humphreys?' said Mrs. Cooper, after a short interval. This was a better opening.

'No, I'm sorry to say I do not,' said Humphreys. 'It seems very pleasant, what I could see of it coming down in the train.'

'Oh, it is a pleasant part. Really, I sometimes say I don't know a nicer district, for the country; and the people round, too: such a quantity always going on. But I'm afraid you've come a little late for some of the better garden parties, Mr. Humphreys.'

'I suppose I have; dear me, what a pity!' said Humphreys, with a gleam of relief; and then, feeling that something more could be got out of this topic, 'But after all, you see, Mrs. Cooper, even if I could have been here earlier, I should have been cut off from them, should I not? My poor uncle's recent death, you know—'

'Oh dear, Mr. Humphreys, to be sure; what a dreadful thing of me to say!' (And Mr. and Miss Cooper seconded the proposition inarticulately.) 'What must you have thought? I am sorry: you must really forgive me.'

'Not at all, Mrs. Cooper, I assure you. I can't honestly assert that my uncle's death was a great grief to me, for I had never seen him. All I meant was that I supposed I shouldn't be expected to take part for some little time in festivities of that kind.'

'Now, really it's very kind of you to take it in that way, Mr. Humphreys, isn't it, George? And you do forgive me?

But only fancy! You never saw poor old Mr. Wilson!'

'Never in my life; nor did I ever have a letter from him. But, by the way, you have something to forgive me for. I've never thanked you, except by letter, for all the trouble you've taken to find people to look after me at the Hall.'

'Oh, I'm sure that was nothing, Mr. Humphreys; but I really do think that you'll find them give satisfaction. The man and his wife whom we've got for the butler and housekeeper we've known for a number of years: such a nice respectable couple, and Mr. Cooper, I'm sure, can answer for the men in the stables and gardens.'

'Yes, Mr. Humphreys, they're a good lot. The head gardener's the only one who's stopped on from Mr. Wilson's time. The major part of the employees, as you no doubt saw by the will, received legacies from the old gentleman and retired from their posts, and as the wife says, your housekeeper and butler are calculated to render you every satisfaction.'

'So everything, Mr. Humphreys, is ready for you to step in this very day, according to what I understood you to wish,' said Mrs. Cooper. 'Everything, that is, except company, and there I'm afraid you'll find yourself quite at a standstill. Only we did understand it was your intention to move in at once. If not, I'm sure you know we should have been only too pleased for you to stay here.'

'I'm quite sure you would, Mrs. Cooper, and I'm very

grateful to you. But I thought I had really better make the plunge at once. I'm accustomed to living alone, and there will be quite enough to occupy my evenings—looking over papers and books and so on—for some time to come, I thought if Mr. Cooper could spare the time this afternoon to go over the house and grounds with me—'

'Certainly, certainly, Mr. Humphreys. My time is your own, up to any hour you please.'

'Till dinner-time, father, you mean,' said Miss Cooper. 'Don't forget we're going over to the Brasnetts'. And have you got all the garden keys?'

'Are you a great gardener, Miss Cooper?' said Mr. Humphreys. 'I wish you would tell me what I'm to expect at the Hall.'

'Oh, I don't know about a great gardener, Mr. Humphreys: I'm very fond of flowers—but the Hall garden might be made quite lovely, I often say. It's very old-fashioned as it is: and a great deal of shrubbery. There's an old temple, besides, and a maze.'

'Really? Have you explored it ever?'

'No-o,' said Miss Cooper, drawing in her lips and shaking her head. 'I've often longed to try, but old Mr. Wilson always kept it locked. He wouldn't even let Lady Wardrop into it. (She lives near here, at Bentley, you know, and she's a great gardener, if you like.) That's why I asked father if he had all the keys.'

'I see. Well, I must evidently look into that, and show you over it when I've learnt the way.'

'Oh, thank you so much, Mr. Humphreys! Now I shall have the laugh of Miss Foster (that's our rector's daughter, you know; they're away on their holiday now—such nice people). We always had a joke between us which should be the first to get into the maze.'

'I think the garden keys must be up at the house,' said Mr. Cooper, who had been looking over a large bunch. 'There is a number there in the library. Now, Mr. Humphreys, if you're prepared, we might bid goodbye to these ladies and set forward on our little tour of exploration.'

As they came out of Mr. Cooper's front gate, Humphreys had to run the gauntlet—not of an organized demonstration, but of a good deal of touching of hats and careful contemplation from the men and women who had gathered in somewhat unusual numbers in the village street. He had, further, to exchange some remarks with the wife of the lodge-keeper as they passed the park gates, and with the lodge-keeper himself, who was attending to the park road. I cannot, however, spare the time to report the progress fully. As they traversed the half-mile or so between the lodge and the house, Humphreys took occasion to ask his companion some question which brought up the topic of his late uncle, and it did not take long before Mr. Cooper was embarked upon a disquisition.

'It is singular to think, as the wife was saying just now, that you should never have seen the old gentleman. And yet—you won't misunderstand me, Mr. Humphreys, I feel confident, when I say that in my opinion there would have been but little congeniality betwixt yourself and him. Not that I have a word to say in deprecation—not a single word. I can tell you what he was,' said Mr. Cooper, pulling up suddenly and fixing Humphreys with his eye. 'Can tell you what he was in a nutshell, as the saying goes. He was a complete, thorough valentudinarian. That describes him to a T. That's what he was, sir, a complete valentudinarian. No participation in what went on around him. I did venture, I think, to send you a few words of cutting from our local paper, which I took the occasion to contribute on his decease. If I recollect myself aright, such is very much the gist of them. But don't, Mr. Humphreys,' continued Cooper, tapping him impressively on the chest,—'don't you run away with the impression that I wish to say aught but what is most creditable—most creditable—of your respected uncle and my late employer. Upright, Mr. Humphreys—open as the day; liberal to all in his dealings. He had the heart to feel and the hand to accommodate. But there it was: there was the stumbling-block—his unfortunate health—or, as I might more truly phrase it, his want of health.'

'Yes, poor man. Did he suffer from any special disorder

before his last illness—which, I take it, was little more than old age?'

'Just that, Mr. Humphreys—just that. The flash flickering slowly away in the pan,' said Cooper, with what he considered an appropriate gesture,—'the golden bowl gradually ceasing to vibrate. But as to your other question I should return a negative answer. General absence of vitality? yes: special complaint? no, unless you reckon a nasty cough he had with him. Why, here we are pretty much at the house. A handsome mansion, Mr. Humphreys, don't you consider?'

It deserved the epithet, on the whole: but it was oddly proportioned—a very tall red-brick house, with a plain parapet concealing the roof almost entirely. It gave the impression of a town house set down in the country; there was a basement, and a rather imposing flight of steps leading up to the front door. It seemed also, owing to its height, to desiderate wings, but there were none. The stables and other offices were concealed by trees. Humphreys guessed its probable date as 1770 or thereabouts.

The mature couple who had been engaged to act as butler and cook-housekeeper were waiting inside the front door, and opened it as their new master approached. Their name, Humphreys already knew, was Calton; of their appearance and manner he formed a favourable impression in the few minutes' talk he had with them. It was agreed that he should go through the plate and the cellar next day with Mr. Calton, and that Mrs. C. should have a talk with him about linen, bedding, and so on—what there was, and what there ought to be. Then he and Cooper, dismissing the Caltons for the present, began their view of the house. Its topography is not of importance to this story. The large rooms on the ground floor were satisfactory, especially the library, which was as large as the dining-room, and had three tall windows facing east. The bedroom prepared for Humphreys was immediately above it. There were many pleasant, and a few really interesting, old pictures. None of the furniture was new, and hardly any of the books were later than the seventies. After hearing of and seeing the few changes his uncle had made in the house, and contemplating a shiny portrait of him which adorned the drawing-room, Humphreys was forced to agree with Cooper that in all probability there would have been little to attract him in his predecessor. It made him rather sad that he could not be sorry—dolebat se dolere non posse—for the man who, whether with or without some feeling of kindliness towards his unknown nephew, had contributed so much to his well-being; for he felt that Wilsthorpe was a place in which he could be happy, and especially happy, it might be, in its library.

And now it was time to go over the garden: the empty stables could wait, and so could the laundry. So to the garden they addressed themselves, and it was soon evident that Miss Cooper had been right in thinking that there were possibilities. Also that Mr. Cooper had done well in keeping on the gardener. The deceased Mr. Wilson might not have, indeed plainly had not, been imbued with the latest views on gardening, but whatever had been done here had been done under the eye of a knowledgeable man, and the equipment and stock were excellent. Cooper was delighted with the pleasure Humphreys showed, and with the suggestions he let fall from time to time. 'I can see,' he said, 'that you've found your meatear here, Mr. Humphreys: you'll make this place a regular signosier before very many seasons have passed over our heads. I wish Clutterham had been here—that's the head gardener—and here he would have been of course, as I told you, but for his son's being horse doover with a fever, poor fellow! I should like him to have heard how the place strikes you.'

'Yes, you told me he couldn't be here today, and I was very sorry to hear the reason, but it will be time enough tomorrow. What is that white building on the mound at the end of the grass ride? Is it the temple Miss Cooper mentioned?'

'That it is, Mr. Humphreys—the Temple of Friendship. Constructed of marble brought out of Italy for the purpose, by your late uncle's grandfather. Would it interest you perhaps to take a turn there? You get a very sweet prospect of the park.'

The general lines of the temple were those of the Sibyl's Temple at Tivoli, helped out by a dome, only the whole was a good deal smaller. Some ancient sepulchral reliefs were built into the wall, and about it all was a pleasant flavour of the grand tour. Cooper produced the key, and with some difficulty opened the heavy door. Inside there was a handsome ceiling, but little furniture. Most of the floor was occupied by a pile of thick circular blocks of stone, each of which had a single letter deeply cut on its slightly convex upper surface. 'What is the meaning of these?' Humphreys inquired.

'Meaning? Well, all things, we're told, have their purpose, Mr. Humphreys, and I suppose these blocks have had theirs as well as another. But what that purpose is or was [Mr. Cooper assumed a didactic attitude here], I, for one, should be at a loss to point out to you, sir. All I know of them— and it's summed up in a very few words—is just this: that they're stated to have been removed by your late uncle, at a period before I entered on the scene, from the maze. That, Mr. Humphreys, is—'

'Oh, the maze!' exclaimed Humphreys. 'I'd forgotten that: we must have a look at it. Where is it?'

Cooper drew him to the door of the temple, and pointed with his stick. 'Guide your eye,' he said (somewhat in the manner of the Second Elder in Handel's 'Susanna'—

Far to the west direct your straining eyes Where yon tall

16

holm-tree rises to the skies)

'Guide your eye by my stick here, and follow out the line directly opposite to the spot where we're standing now, and I'll engage, Mr. Humphreys, that you'll catch the archway over the entrance. You'll see it just at the end of the walk answering to the one that leads up to this very building. Did you think of going there at once? because if that be the case, I must go to the house and procure the key. If you would walk on there, I'll rejoin you in a few moments' time.'

Accordingly Humphreys strolled down the ride leading to the temple, past the garden-front of the house, and up the turfy approach to the archway which Cooper had pointed out to him. He was surprised to find that the whole maze was surrounded by a high wall, and that the archway was provided with a padlocked iron gate; but then he remembered that Miss Cooper had spoken of his uncle's objection to letting anyone enter this part of the garden. He was now at the gate, and still Cooper came not. For a few minutes he occupied himself in reading the motto cut over the entrance, Secretum meum mihi et filiis domus meae, and in trying to recollect the source of it. Then he became impatient and considered the possibility of scaling the wall. This was clearly not worth while; it might have been done if he had been wearing an older suit: or could the padlock—a very old one—be forced? No, apparently not: and yet, as he gave a final irritated kick at the gate, something gave way, and the lock fell at his feet.

He pushed the gate open inconveniencing a number of nettles as he did so, and stepped into the enclosure.

It was a yew maze, of circular form, and the hedges, long untrimmed, had grown out and upwards to a most unorthodox breadth and height. The walks, too, were next door to impassable. Only by entirely disregarding scratches, nettle-stings, and wet, could Humphreys force his way along them; but at any rate this condition of things, he reflected, would make it easier for him to find his way out again, for he left a very visible track. So far as he could remember, he had never been in a maze before, nor did it seem to him now that he had missed much. The dankness and darkness, and smell of crushed goosegrass and nettles were anything but cheerful. Still, it did not seem to be a very intricate specimen of its kind. Here he was (by the way, was that Cooper arrived at last? No!) very nearly at the heart of it, without having taken much thought as to what path he was following. Ah! there at last was the centre, easily gained. And there was something to reward him. His first impression was that the central ornament was a sundial; but when he had switched away some portion of the thick growth of brambles and bindweed that had formed over it, he saw that it was a less ordinary decoration. A stone column about four feet high, and on the top of it a metal globe—copper, to judge by the green patina—engraved, and finely engraved too, with figures in outline, and letters. That was what Humphreys saw, and a brief glance at the figures convinced him that it was one of those mysterious things called celestial globes, from which, one would suppose, no one ever yet derived any information about the heavens. However, it was too dark—at least in the maze—for him to examine this curiosity at all closely, and besides, he now heard Cooper's voice, and sounds as of an elephant in the jungle. Humphreys called to him to follow the track he had beaten out, and soon Cooper emerged panting into the central circle. He was full of apologies for his delay; he had not been able, after all, to find the key. 'But there!' he said, 'you've penetrated into the heart of the mystery unaided and unannealed, as the saying goes. Well! I suppose it's a matter of thirty to forty years since any human foot has trod these precincts. Certain it is that I've never set foot in them before. Well, well! what's the old proverb about angels fearing to tread? It's proved true once again in this case.' Humphreys' acquaintance with Cooper, though it had been short, was sufficient to assure him that there was no guile in this allusion, and he forbore the obvious remark, merely suggesting that it was fully time to get back to the house for a late cup of tea, and to release Cooper for his evening engagement. They left the maze accordingly, experiencing well-nigh the same ease in retracing their path as they had in coming in.

'Have you any idea,' Humphreys asked, as they went towards the house, 'why my uncle kept that place so carefully locked?'

Cooper pulled up, and Humphreys felt that he must be on the brink of a revelation.

'I should merely be deceiving you, Mr. Humphreys, and that to no good purpose, if I laid claim to possess any information whatsoever on that topic. When I first entered upon my duties here, some eighteen years back, that maze was word for word in the condition you see it now, and the one and only occasion on which the question ever arose within my knowledge was that of which my girl made mention in your hearing. Lady Wardrop—I've not a word to say against her—wrote applying for admission to the maze. Your uncle showed me the note—a most civil note—everything that could be expected from such a quarter. 'Cooper,' he said, 'I wish you'd reply to that note on my behalf.' 'Certainly Mr. Wilson,' I said, for I was quite inured to acting as his secretary, 'what answer shall I return to it?' 'Well,' he said, 'give Lady Wardrop my compliments, and tell her that if ever that portion of the grounds is taken in hand I shall be happy to give her the first opportunity of viewing it, but that it has been shut up now for a number of years, and I shall be grateful to her if she kindly won't press the matter.' That, Mr. Humphreys, was your good uncle's last word on the subject, and I don't think I can add anything to it. Unless,' added Cooper, after a pause, 'it might be just this: that, so far as I could form a judgement, he had a dislike (as people often will for one reason or another) to the memory of his grandfather, who, as I mentioned to you, had that maze laid out. A man of peculiar teenets, Mr. Humphreys, and a great traveller. You'll have the opportunity, on the coming Sabbath, of seeing the tablet to him in our little parish church; put up it was some long time after his death.'

'Oh! I should have expected a man who had such a taste for building to have designed a mausoleum for himself.'

'Well, I've never noticed anything of the kind you mention; and, in fact, come to think of it, I'm not at all sure that his resting-place is within our boundaries at all: that he lays in the vault I'm pretty confident is not the case. Curious now that I shouldn't be in a position to inform you on that heading! Still, after all, we can't say, can we, Mr. Humphreys, that it's a point of crucial importance where the pore mortal coils are bestowed?'

At this point they entered the house, and Cooper's speculations were interrupted.

Tea was laid in the library, where Mr. Cooper fell upon subjects appropriate to the scene. 'A fine collection of books! One of the finest, I've understood from connoisseurs, in this part of the country; splendid plates, too, in some of these works. I recollect your uncle showing me one with views of foreign towns—most absorbing it was: got up in first-rate style. And another all done by hand, with the ink as fresh as if it had been laid on yesterday, and yet, he told me, it was the work of some old monk hundreds of years back. I've always taken a keen interest in literature myself. Hardly anything to my mind can compare with a good hour's reading after a hard day's work; far better than wasting the whole evening at a friend's house—and that reminds me, to be sure. I shall be getting into trouble with the wife if I don't make the best of my way home and get ready to squander away one of these same evenings! I must be off, Mr. Humphreys.'

'And that reminds me,' said Humphreys, 'if I'm to show Miss Cooper the maze tomorrow we must have it cleared out a bit. Could you say a word about that to the proper person?'

'Why, to be sure. A couple of men with scythes could cut out a track tomorrow morning. I'll leave word as I pass the lodge, and I'll tell them, what'll save you the trouble, perhaps, Mr. Humphreys, of having to go up and extract them yourself: that they'd better have some sticks or a tape to mark out their way with as they go on.'

'A very good idea! Yes, do that; and I'll expect Mrs. and Miss Cooper in the afternoon, and yourself about half-past ten in the morning.'

'It'll be a pleasure, I'm sure, both to them and to myself, Mr. Humphreys. Good night!'

Humphreys dined at eight. But for the fact that it was his first evening, and that Calton was evidently inclined for occasional conversation, he would have finished the novel he had bought for his journey. As it was, he had to listen and reply to some of Calton's impressions of the neighbourhood and the season: the latter, it appeared, was seasonable, and the former had changed considerably—and not altogether for the worse—since Calton's boyhood (which had been spent there). The village shop in particular had greatly improved since the year 1870. It was now possible to procure there pretty much anything you liked in reason: which was a conveniency, because suppose anythink was required of a suddent (and he had known such things before now), he (Calton) could step down there (supposing the shop to be still open), and order it in, without he borrered it of the Rectory, whereas in earlier days it would have been useless to pursue such a course in respect of anything but candles, or soap, or treacle, or perhaps a penny child's picture-book, and nine times out of ten it'd be something more in the nature of a bottle of whisky you'd be requiring; leastways—On the whole Humphreys thought he would be prepared with a book in future.

The library was the obvious place for the after-dinner hours. Candle in hand and pipe in mouth, he moved round the room for some time, taking stock of the titles of the books. He had all the predisposition to take interest in an old library, and there was every opportunity for him here to make systematic acquaintance with one, for he had learned from Cooper that there was no catalogue save the very superficial one made for purposes of probate. The drawing up of a catalogue raisonné would be a delicious occupation for winter. There were probably treasures to be found, too: even manuscripts, if Cooper might be trusted.

As he pursued his round the sense came upon him (as it does upon most of us in similar places) of the extreme unreadableness of a great portion of the collection. 'Editions of Classics and Fathers, and Picart's Religious Ceremonies, and the Harleian Miscellany, I suppose are all very well, but who is ever going to read Tostatus Abulensis, or Pineda on Job, or a book like this?' He picked out a small quarto, loose in the binding, and from which the lettered label had fallen off; and observing that coffee was waiting for him, retired to a chair. Eventually he opened the book. It will be observed that his condemnation of it rested wholly on external grounds. For all he knew it might have been a collection of unique plays, but undeniably the outside was blank and forbidding. As a matter of fact, it was a collection of sermons or meditations, and mutilated at that, for the first sheet was gone. It seemed to belong to the latter end of the seventeenth century. He turned over the pages till his eye was caught by a marginal note: 'A Parable of this Unhappy Condition,' and he thought he would see what aptitudes the author might have for imaginative composition. 'I have heard or read,' so ran the passage, 'whether in the way of Parable or true

Relation I leave my Reader to judge, of a Man who, like Theseus, in the Attick Tale, should adventure himself, into a Labyrinth or Maze: and such an one indeed as was not laid out in the Fashion of our Topiary artists of this Age, but of a wide compass, in which, moreover, such unknown Pitfalls and Snares, nay, such ill-omened Inhabitants were commonly thought to lurk as could only be encountered at the Hazard of one's very life. Now you may be sure that in such a Case the Disswasions of Friends were not wanting. 'Consider of such-an-one' says a Brother 'how he went the way you wot of, and was never seen more.' 'Or of such another' says the Mother 'that adventured himself but a little way in, and from that day forth is so troubled in his Wits that he cannot tell what he saw, nor hath passed one good Night.' 'And have you never heard' cries a Neighbour 'of what Faces have been seen to look out over the Palisadoes and betwixt the Bars of the Gate?' But all would not do: the Man was set upon his Purpose: for it seems it was the common fireside Talk of that Country that at the Heart and Centre of this Labyrinth there was a Jewel of such Price and Rarity that would enrich the Finder thereof for his life: and this should be his by right that could persever to come at it. What then? Quid multa? The Adventurer pass'd the Gates, and for a whole day's space his Friends without had no news of him, except it might be by some indistinct Cries heard afar off in the Night, such as made them turn in their restless Beds and sweat for very

Fear, not doubting but that their Son and Brother had put one more to the Catalogue of those unfortunates that had suffer'd shipwreck on that Voyage. So the next day they went with weeping Tears to the Clark of the Parish to order the Bell to be toll'd. And their Way took them hard by the gate of the Labyrinth: which they would have hastened by, from the Horrour they had of it, but that they caught sight of a sudden of a Man's Body lying in the Roadway, and going up to it (with what Anticipations may be easily figured) found it to be him whom they reckoned as lost: and not dead, though he were in a Swound most like Death. They then, who had gone forth as Mourners came back rejoycing, and set to by all means to revive their Prodigal. Who, being come to himself, and hearing of their Anxieties and their Errand of that Morning, 'Ay' says he 'you may as well finish what you were about: for, for all I have brought back the Jewel (which he shew'd them, and 'twas indeed a rare Piece) I have brought back that with it that will leave me neither Rest at Night nor Pleasure by Day.' Whereupon they were instant with him to learn his Meaning, and where his Company should be that went so sore against his Stomach. 'O' says he ' 'tis here in my Breast: I cannot flee from it, do what I may.' So it needed no Wizard to help them to a guess that it was the Recollection of what he had seen that troubled him so wonderfully. But they could get no more of him for a long Time but by Fits and Starts. However at long and at last they made shift to collect somewhat of this kind: that at first, while the Sun was bright, he went merrily on, and without any Difficulty reached the Heart of the Labyrinth and got the Jewel, and so set out on his way back rejoycing: but as the Night fell, wherein all the Beasts of the Forest do move, he begun to be sensible of some Creature keeping Pace with him and, as he thought, peering and looking upon him from the next Alley to that he was in; and that when he should stop, this Companion should stop also, which put him in some Disorder of his Spirits. And, indeed, as the Darkness increas'd, it seemed to him that there was more than one, and, it might be, even a whole Band of such Followers: at least so he judg'd by the Rustling and Cracking that they kept among the Thickets; besides that there would be at a Time a Sound of Whispering, which seem'd to import a Conference among them. But in regard of who they were or what Form they were of, he would not be persuaded to say what he thought. Upon his Hearers asking him what the Cries were which they heard in the Night (as was observ'd above) he gave them this Account: That about Midnight (so far as he could judge) he heard his Name call'd from a long way off, and he would have been sworn it was his Brother that so call'd him. So he stood still and hilloo'd at the Pitch of his Voice, and he suppos'd that the Echo, or the Noyse of his Shouting, disguis'd for the Moment any lesser sound; because, when there fell a Stillness again, he

27

distinguish'd a Trampling (not loud) of running Feet coming
very close behind him, wherewith he was so daunted that
himself set off to run, and that he continued till the Dawn
broke. Sometimes when his Breath fail'd him, he would cast
himself flat on his Face, and hope that his Pursuers might
over-run him in the Darkness, but at such a Time they
would regularly make a Pause, and he could hear them pant
and snuff as it had been a Hound at Fault: which wrought
in him so extream an Horrour of mind, that he would be
forc'd to betake himself again to turning and doubling, if
by any Means he might throw them off the Scent. And, as if
this Exertion was in itself not terrible enough, he had before
him the constant Fear of falling into some Pit or Trap, of
which he had heard, and indeed seen with his own Eyes
that there were several, some at the sides and other in the
Midst of the Alleys. So that in fine (he said) a more dreadful
Night was never spent by Mortal Creature than that he had
endur'd in that Labyrinth; and not that Jewel which he had
in his Wallet, nor the richest that was ever brought out of
the Indies, could be a sufficient Recompence to him for the
Pains he had suffered.

'I will spare to set down the further Recital of this
Man's Troubles, inasmuch as I am confident my Reader's
Intelligence will hit the Parallel I desire to draw. For is not
this Jewel a just Emblem of the Satisfaction which a Man
may bring back with him from a Course of this World's

Pleasures? and will not the Labyrinth serve for an Image of the World itself wherein such a Treasure (if we may believe the common Voice) is stored up?'

At about this point Humphreys thought that a little Patience would be an agreeable change, and that the writer's 'improvement' of his Parable might be left to itself. So he put the book back in its former place, wondering as he did so whether his uncle had ever stumbled across that passage; and if so, whether it had worked on his fancy so much as to make him dislike the idea of a maze, and determine to shut up the one in the garden. Not long afterwards he went to bed.

The next day brought a morning's hard work with Mr. Cooper, who, if exuberant in language, had the business of the estate at his fingers' ends. He was very breezy this morning, Mr. Cooper was: had not forgotten the order to clear out the maze—the work was going on at that moment: his girl was on the tentacles of expectation about it. He also hoped that Humphreys had slept the sleep of the just, and that we should be favoured with a continuance of this congenial weather. At luncheon he enlarged on the pictures in the dining-room, and pointed out the portrait of the constructor of the temple and the maze. Humphreys examined this with considerable interest. It was the work of an Italian, and had been painted when old Mr. Wilson was visiting Rome as a young man. (There was, indeed, a

29

view of the Colosseum in the background.) A pale thin face
and large eyes were the characteristic features. In the hand
was a partially unfolded roll of paper, on which could be
distinguished the plan of a circular building, very probably
the temple, and also part of that of a labyrinth. Humphreys
got up on a chair to examine it, but it was not painted with
sufficient clearness to be worth copying. It suggested to him,
however, that he might as well make a plan of his own maze
and hang it in the hall for the use of visitors.

This determination of his was confirmed that same
afternoon; for when Mrs. and Miss Cooper arrived, eager
to be inducted into the maze, he found that he was wholly
unable to lead them to the centre. The gardeners had removed
the guide-marks they had been using, and even Clutterham,
when summoned to assist, was as helpless as the rest. 'The
point is, you see, Mr. Wilson—I should say 'Umphreys—
these mazes is purposely constructed so much alike, with a
view to mislead. Still, if you'll foller me, I think I can put you
right. I'll just put my 'at down 'ere as a starting-point.' He
stumped off, and after five minutes brought the party safe
to the hat again. 'Now that's a very peculiar thing,' he said,
with a sheepish laugh. 'I made sure I'd left that 'at just over
against a bramble-bush, and you can see for yourself there
ain't no bramble-bush not in this walk at all. If you'll allow
me, Mr. Humphreys—that's the name, ain't it, sir?—I'll just
call one of the men in to mark the place like.'

William Crack arrived, in answer to repeated shouts. He had some difficulty in making his way to the party. First he was seen or heard in an inside alley, then, almost at the same moment, in an outer one. However, he joined them at last, and was first consulted without effect and then stationed by the hat, which Clutterham still considered it necessary to leave on the ground. In spite of this strategy, they spent the best part of three-quarters of an hour in quite fruitless wanderings, and Humphreys was obliged at last, seeing how tired Mrs. Cooper was becoming, to suggest a retreat to tea, with profuse apologies to Miss Cooper. 'At any rate you've won your bet with Miss Foster,' he said; 'you have been inside the maze; and I promise you the first thing I do shall be to make a proper plan of it with the lines marked out for you to go by.' 'That's what's wanted, sir,' said Clutterham, 'someone to draw out a plan and keep it by them. It might be very awkward, you see, anyone getting into that place and a shower of rain come on, and them not able to find their way out again; it might be hours before they could be got out, without you'd permit of me makin' a short cut to the middle: what my meanin' is, takin' down a couple of trees in each 'edge in a straight line so as you could git a clear view right through. Of course that'd do away with it as a maze, but I don't know as you'd approve of that.'

'No, I won't have that done yet: I'll make a plan first, and let you have a copy. Later on, if we find occasion, I'll think of what you say.'

Humphreys was vexed and ashamed at the fiasco of the afternoon, and could not be satisfied without making another effort that evening to reach the centre of the maze. His irritation was increased by finding it without a single false step. He had thoughts of beginning his plan at once; but the light was fading, and he felt that by the time he had got the necessary materials together, work would be impossible.

Next morning accordingly, carrying a drawing-board, pencils, compasses, cartridge paper, and so forth (some of which had been borrowed from the Coopers and some found in the library cupboards), he went to the middle of the maze (again without any hesitation), and set out his materials. He was, however, delayed in making a start. The brambles and weeds that had obscured the column and globe were now all cleared away, and it was for the first time possible to see clearly what these were like. The column was featureless, resembling those on which sundials are usually placed. Not so the globe. I have said that it was finely engraved with figures and inscriptions, and that on a first glance Humphreys had taken it for a celestial globe: but he soon found that it did not answer to his recollection of such things. One feature seemed familiar; a winged serpent— Draco—encircled it about the place which, on a terrestrial globe, is occupied by the equator: but on the other hand, a good part of the upper hemisphere was covered by the outspread wings of a large figure whose head was concealed by a ring at the pole or summit of the whole. Around the place of the head the words princeps tenebrarum could be deciphered. In the lower hemisphere there was a space hatched all over with cross-lines and marked as umbra mortis. Near it was a range of mountains, and among them a valley with flames rising from it. This was lettered (will you be surprised to learn it?) vallis filiorum Hinnom. Above and below Draco were outlined various figures not unlike the pictures of the ordinary constellations, but not the same. Thus, a nude man with a raised club was described, not as Hercules but as Cain. Another, plunged up to his middle in earth and stretching out despairing arms, was Chore, not Ophiuchus, and a third, hung by his hair to a snaky tree, was Absolon. Near the last, a man in long robes and high cap, standing in a circle and addressing two shaggy demons who hovered outside, was described as Hostanes magus (a character unfamiliar to Humphreys). The scheme of the whole, indeed, seemed to be an assemblage of the patriarchs of evil, perhaps not uninfluenced by a study of Dante. Humphreys thought it an unusual exhibition of his great-grandfather's taste, but reflected that he had probably picked it up in Italy and had never taken the trouble to examine it closely: certainly, had he set much store by it, he would not have exposed it to wind and weather. He tapped the metal—

it seemed hollow and not very thick—and, turning from it, addressed himself to his plan. After half an hour's work he found it was impossible to get on without using a clue: so he procured a roll of twine from Clutterham, and laid it out along the alleys from the entrance to the centre, tying the end to the ring at the top of the globe. This expedient helped him to set out a rough plan before luncheon, and in the afternoon he was able to draw it in more neatly. Towards tea-time Mr. Cooper joined him, and was much interested in his progress. 'Now this—' said Mr. Cooper, laying his hand on the globe, and then drawing it away hastily. 'Whew! Holds the heat, doesn't it, to a surprising degree, Mr. Humphreys. I suppose this metal—copper, isn't it?—would be an insulator or conductor, or whatever they call it.'

'The sun has been pretty strong this afternoon,' said Humphreys, evading the scientific point, 'but I didn't notice the globe had got hot. No—it doesn't seem very hot to me,' he added.

'Odd!' said Mr. Cooper. 'Now I can't hardly bear my hand on it. Something in the difference of temperament between us, I suppose. I dare say you're a chilly subject, Mr. Humphreys: I'm not: and there's where the distinction lies. All this summer I've slept, if you'll believe me, practically in statu quo, and had my morning tub as cold as I could get it. Day out and day in-let me assist you with that string.'

'It's all right, thanks; but if you'll collect some of these pencils and things that are lying about I shall be much obliged. Now I think we've got everything, and we might get back to the house.'

They left the maze, Humphreys rolling up the clue as they went.

The night was rainy.

Most unfortunately it turned out that, whether by Cooper's fault or not, the plan had been the one thing forgotten the evening before. As was to be expected, it was ruined by the wet. There was nothing for it but to begin again (the job would not be a long one this time). The clue therefore was put in place once more and a fresh start made. But Humphreys had not done much before an interruption came in the shape of Calton with a telegram. His late chief in London wanted to consult him. Only a brief interview was wanted, but the summons was urgent. This was annoying, yet it was not really upsetting; there was a train available in half an hour, and, unless things went very cross, he could be back, possibly by five o'clock, certainly by eight. He gave the plan to Calton to take to the house, but it was not worth while to remove the clue.

All went as he had hoped. He spent a rather exciting evening in the library, for he lighted tonight upon a cupboard where some of the rarer books were kept. When he went up to bed he was glad to find that the servant had remembered to leave his curtains undrawn and his windows open. He put down his light, and went to the window which commanded a view of the garden and the park. It was a brilliant moonlight night. In a few weeks' time the sonorous winds of autumn would break up all this calm. But now the distant woods were in a deep stillness; the slopes of the lawns were shining with dew; the colours of some of the flowers could almost be guessed. The light of the moon just caught the cornice of the temple and the curve of its leaden dome, and Humphreys had to own that, so seen, these conceits of a past age have a real beauty. In short, the light, the perfume of the woods, and the absolute quiet called up such kind old associations in his mind that he went on ruminating them for a long, long time. As he turned from the window he felt he had never seen anything more complete of its sort. The one feature that struck him with a sense of incongruity was a small Irish yew, thin and black, which stood out like an outpost of the shrubbery, through which the maze was approached. That, he thought, might as well be away: the wonder was that anyone should have thought it would look well in that position.

However, next morning, in the press of answering letters and going over books with Mr. Cooper, the Irish yew was forgotten. One letter, by the way, arrived this day which has to be mentioned. It was from that Lady Wardrop whom Miss Cooper had mentioned, and it renewed the application which she had addressed to Mr. Wilson. She pleaded, in the first place, that she was about to publish a Book of Mazes, and earnestly desired to include the plan of the Wilsthorpe Maze, and also that it would be a great kindness if Mr. Humphreys could let her see it (if at all) at an early date, since she would soon have to go abroad for the winter months. Her house at Bentley was not far distant, so Humphreys was able to send a note by hand to her suggesting the very next day or the day after for her visit; it may be said at once that the messenger brought back a most grateful answer, to the effect that the morrow would suit her admirably.

The only other event of the day was that the plan of the maze was successfully finished.

This night again was fair and brilliant and calm, and Humphreys lingered almost as long at his window. The Irish yew came to his mind again as he was on the point of drawing his curtains: but either he had been misled by a shadow the night before, or else the shrub was not really so obtrusive as he had fancied. Anyhow, he saw no reason for interfering with it. What he would do away with, however, was a clump of dark growth which had usurped a place against the house wall, and was threatening to obscure one of the lower range of windows. It did not look as if it could possibly be worth keeping; he fancied it dank and unhealthy, little as he could see of it.

Next day (it was a Friday—he had arrived at Wilsthorpe

on a Monday) Lady Wardrop came over in her car soon after luncheon. She was a stout elderly person, very full of talk of all sorts and particularly inclined to make herself agreeable to Humphreys, who had gratified her very much by his ready granting of her request. They made a thorough exploration of the place together; and Lady Wardrop's opinion of her host obviously rose sky-high when she found that he really knew something of gardening. She entered enthusiastically into all his plans for improvement, but agreed that it would be a vandalism to interfere with the characteristic laying-out of the ground near the house. With the temple she was particularly delighted, and, said she, 'Do you know, Mr. Humphreys, I think your bailiff must be right about those lettered blocks of stone. One of my mazes—I'm sorry to say the stupid people have destroyed it now—it was at a place in Hampshire—had the track marked out in that way. They were tiles there, but lettered just like yours, and the letters, taken in the right order, formed an inscription—what it was I forget—something about Theseus and Ariadne. I have a copy of it, as well as the plan of the maze where it was. How people can do such things! I shall never forgive you if you injure your maze. Do you know, they're becoming very uncommon? Almost every year I hear of one being grubbed up. Now, do let's get straight to it: or, if you're too busy, I know my way there perfectly, and I'm not afraid of getting lost in it; I know too much about mazes for that. Though I

remember missing my lunch—not so very long ago either—
through getting entangled in the one at Busbury. Well, of
course, if you can manage to come with me, that will be all
the nicer.'

After this confident prelude justice would seem to
require that Lady Wardrop should have been hopelessly
muddled by the Wilsthorpe maze. Nothing of that kind
happened: yet it is to be doubted whether she got all the
enjoyment from her new specimen that she expected. She
was interested—keenly interested—to be sure, and pointed
out to Humphreys a series of little depressions in the ground
which, she thought, marked the places of the lettered blocks.
She told him, too, what other mazes resembled his most
closely in arrangement, and explained how it was usually
possible to date a maze to within twenty years by means of
its plan. This one, she already knew, must be about as old as
1780, and its features were just what might be expected. The
globe, furthermore, completely absorbed her. It was unique
in her experience, and she pored over it for long. 'I should
like a rubbing of that,' she said, 'if it could possibly be
made. Yes, I am sure you would be most kind about it, Mr.
Humphreys, but I trust you won't attempt it on my account,
I do indeed; I shouldn't like to take any liberties here. I have
the feeling that it might be resented. Now, confess,' she went
on, turning and facing Humphreys, 'don't you feel—haven't
you felt ever since you came in here—that a watch is being

kept on us, and that if we overstepped the mark in any way there would be a—well, a pounce? No? I do; and I don't care how soon we are outside the gate.'

'After all,' she said, when they were once more on their way to the house, 'it may have been only the airlessness and the dull heat of that place that pressed on my brain. Still, I'll take back one thing I said. I'm not sure that I shan't forgive you after all, if I find next spring that that maze has been grubbed up.'

'Whether or no that's done, you shall have the plan, Lady Wardrop. I have made one, and no later than tonight I can trace you a copy.'

'Admirable: a pencil tracing will be all I want, with an indication of the scale. I can easily have it brought into line with the rest of my plates. Many, many thanks.'

'Very well, you shall have that tomorrow. I wish you could help me to a solution of my block-puzzle.'

'What, those stones in the summer-house? That is a puzzle; they are in no sort of order? Of course not. But the men who put them down must have had some directions— perhaps you'll find a paper about it among your uncle's things. If not, you'll have to call in somebody who's an expert in ciphers.'

'Advise me about something else, please,' said Humphreys. 'That bush-thing under the library window: you would have that away, wouldn't you?'

'Which? That? Oh, I think not,' said Lady Wardrop. 'I can't see it very well from this distance, but it's not unsightly.'

'Perhaps you're right; only, looking out of my window, just above it, last night, I thought it took up too much room. It doesn't seem to, as one sees it from here, certainly. Very well, I'll leave it alone for a bit.'

Tea was the next business, soon after which Lady Wardrop drove off; but, half-way down the drive, she stopped the car and beckoned to Humphreys, who was still on the front-door steps. He ran to glean her parting words, which were: 'It just occurs to me, it might be worth your while to look at the underside of those stones. They must have been numbered, mustn't they? Good-bye again. Home, please.'

The main occupation of this evening at any rate was settled. The tracing of the plan for Lady Wardrop and the careful collation of it with the original meant a couple of hours' work at least. Accordingly, soon after nine Humphreys had his materials put out in the library and began. It was a still, stuffy evening; windows had to stand open, and he had more than one grisly encounter with a bat. These unnerving episodes made him keep the tail of his eye on the window. Once or twice it was a question whether there was—not a bat, but something more considerable—that had a mind to join him. How unpleasant it would be if someone had

41

slipped noiselessly over the sill and was crouching on the floor!

The tracing of the plan was done: it remained to compare it with the original, and to see whether any paths had been wrongly closed or left open. With one finger on each paper, he traced out the course that must be followed from the entrance. There were one or two slight mistakes, but here, near the centre, was a bad confusion, probably due to the entry of the Second or Third Bat. Before correcting the copy he followed out carefully the last turnings of the path on the original. These, at least, were right; they led without a hitch to the middle space. Here was a feature which need not be repeated on the copy—an ugly black spot about the size of a shilling. Ink? No. It resembled a hole, but how should a hole be there? He stared at it with tired eyes: the work of tracing had been very laborious, and he was drowsy and oppressed... But surely this was a very odd hole. It seemed to go not only through the paper, but through the table on which it lay. Yes, and through the floor below that, down, and still down, even into infinite depths. He craned over it, utterly bewildered. Just as, when you were a child, you may have pored over a square inch of counterpane until it became a landscape with wooded hills, and perhaps even churches and houses, and you lost all thought of the true size of yourself and it, so this hole seemed to Humphreys for the moment the only thing in the world. For some reason it was hateful to him from the first, but he had gazed at it for some moments before any feeling of anxiety came upon him; and then it did come, stronger and stronger—a horror lest something might emerge from it, and a really agonizing conviction that a terror was on its way, from the sight of which he would not be able to escape. Oh yes, far, far down there was a movement, and the movement was upwards—towards the surface. Nearer and nearer it came, and it was of a blackish-grey colour with more than one dark hole. It took shape as a face—a human face—a burnt human face: and with the odious writhings of a wasp creeping out of a rotten apple there clambered forth an appearance of a form, waving black arms prepared to clasp the head that was bending over them. With a convulsion of despair Humphreys threw himself back, struck his head against a hanging lamp, and fell.

There was concussion of the brain, shock to the system, and a long confinement to bed. The doctor was badly puzzled, not by the symptoms, but by a request which Humphreys made to him as soon as he was able to say anything. 'I wish you would open the ball in the maze.' 'Hardly room enough there, I should have thought,' was the best answer he could summon up; 'but it's more in your way than mine; my dancing days are over.' At which Humphreys muttered and turned over to sleep, and the doctor intimated to the nurses that the patient was not out of the wood yet. When he was better able to express his views, Humphreys made his meaning clear, and received a promise that the thing should be done at once. He was so anxious to learn the result that the doctor, who seemed a little pensive next morning, saw that more harm than good would be done by saving up his report. 'Well,' he said, 'I am afraid the ball is done for; the metal must have worn thin, I suppose. Anyhow, it went all to bits with the first blow of the chisel.' 'Well? go on, do!' said Humphreys impatiently. 'Oh! you want to know what we found in it, of course. Well, it was half full of stuff like ashes.' 'Ashes? What did you make of them?' 'I haven't thoroughly examined them yet; there's hardly been time: but Cooper's made up his mind—I dare say from something I said—that it's a case of cremation... Now don't excite yourself, my good sir: yes, I must allow I think he's probably right.'

The maze is gone, and Lady Wardrop has forgiven Humphreys; in fact, I believe he married her niece. She was right, too, in her conjecture that the stones in the temple were numbered. There had been a numeral painted on the bottom of each. Some few of these had rubbed off, but enough remained to enable Humphreys to reconstruct the inscription. It ran thus:

PENETRANS AD INTERIORA MORTIS

Grateful as Humphreys was to the memory of his uncle,

he could not quite forgive him for having burnt the journals and letters of the James Wilson who had gifted Wilsthorpe with the maze and the temple. As to the circumstances of that ancestor's death and burial no tradition survived; but his will, which was almost the only record of him accessible, assigned an unusually generous legacy to a servant who bore an Italian name.

Mr. Cooper's view is that, humanly speaking, all these many solemn events have a meaning for us, if our limited intelligence permitted of our disintegrating it, while Mr. Calton has been reminded of an aunt now gone from us, who, about the year 1866, had been lost for upwards of an hour and a half in the maze at Covent Gardens, or it might be Hampton Court.

One of the oddest things in the whole series of transactions is that the book which contained the Parable has entirely disappeared. Humphreys has never been able to find it since he copied out the passage to send to Lady Wardrop.

www.ingramcontent.com/pod-product-compliance
Lightning Source LLC
Chambersburg PA
CBHW030241180626
46810CB00008B/3232